This hook book belongs to

_____

_____

For Dr Mohan Rao. For Achala and Pratya.
Part of me. —Adithi

For Sarthak, a boy who loved animals. —Aaryama

DUCKBILL BOOKS

USA | Canada | UK | Ireland | Australia
New Zealand | India | South Africa | China

Duckbill Books is part of the Penguin Random House group of companies
whose addresses can be found at global.penguinrandomhouse.com

Published by Penguin Random House India Pvt. Ltd
4th Floor, Capital Tower 1, MG Road,
Gurugram 122 002, Haryana, India

Penguin
Random House
India

First published in Duckbill Books by
Penguin Random House India 2021

ISBN 9780143452379

Typeset in Century

Printed at Aarvee Promotions, India

www.penguin.co.in

BOY, BEAR

ADITHI RAO

illustrations by Aaryama Somayaji

An imprint of Penguin Random House

Bear is big. Boy is not so big.

Even Bear was not always big.

Once, Little Bear had travelled from his home in the forest all the way to Mumbai in a tiny box.

Boy's baba was a madari. He bought Bear and trained him to dance.

How did Baba train Bear to dance?

He put Little Bear on a metal plate. He played the dumroo. Little Bear hopped because the plate was very hot. Soon, hot plates and dumroos came to mean the same thing to Little Bear. Now, when a dumroo plays, Bear hops in fright.

It looks like dancing.

People love to watch. They drop coins into Baba's bowl.

CLINK!

CLINK!

CLINK!

Boy and Bear never speak. They never play together.

Bear eats bread. Boy eats whatever Baba brings him each night.

They sleep under a tarpaulin on the sidewalk.

When Boy has bad dreams, Baba pats him back to sleep.

Now Baba is gone. Boy sits on the wall and looks out at the sea sadly . . .

Where is Bear?

He is looking out at the sea too.

There's money left in Baba's bowl. Boy buys bread for Bear and vada pav for himself.

The next morning, he tugs at Bear's chain. Bear follows Boy outside.

Boy plays the dumroo. Bear dances. Coins fill the bowl.

CLINK!   CLINK!   CLINK!

The days go by.

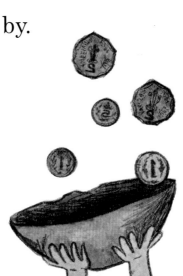

One night, Boy dreams of Baba. He cries. Someone pats him back to sleep.

In the morning, Boy wakes up with his arms around Bear.

When Boy tugs on Bear's chain, Bear flinches.

Gently, Boy removes the ring from Bear's nose. Bear sits very still while he does this.

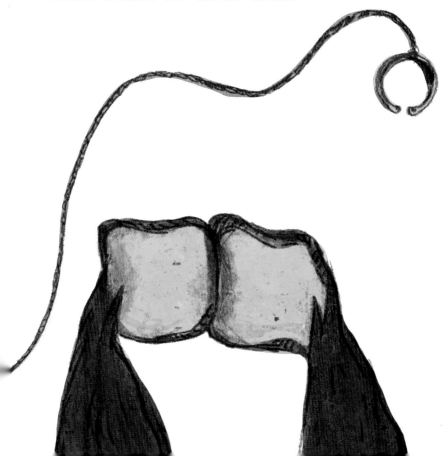

It is Sunday. Lots of tourists. Many dancing bears. Along the sea wall, bowls fill quickly with coins.

CLINK! CLINK! CLINK!

That night, Boy buys fish kebabs and naan. Yummy! He gobbles down his dinner.

Bear doesn't touch his. Boy remembers that Bear's teeth are broken. He can only eat bread.

Are all bears born with broken teeth? Boy gently strokes Bear's snout. Bear sits very still as he does this.

The next day, the madaris
are frightened.

'Hide!' they cry. 'The wildlife people have come to take away our bears!'

Within seconds, the sidewalk is empty. Baba had always made sure Bear was never caught. Baba always saved Bear!

Inside the hut, Boy and Bear huddle quietly together.

Boy watches Bear. He looks sad. He looks like a sad, tired old bear.

Dancing Bear.

DUM DUM DUM!

HOP HOP HOP!

Now Boy knows that it is his
turn to save Bear.

CLINK!

He crawls out from under the tarpaulin. Bear looks away. Only the white corners of his eyes are visible. Boy extends his hand and leaves it there for a long time. Slowly, Bear puts his paw into it.

On the footpath, the wildlife people stop and stare. Boy walks up to a lady. He puts Bear's paw into her hand.

'Ali!' she calls. 'Come quickly. Take the animal.'

Boy and Bear look at each
other silently. Then, Ali takes
Bear away.

The woman's arm comes around Boy's shoulder. 'Have you ever been to school?' she asks gently.

Boy shakes his head. His eyes are on the furry face visible at the back of the wildlife van.

The face grows smaller and smaller as the van pulls away.

'Maybe you will join our team someday,' the wildlife lady smiles.

And Boy feels his heart lift at the thought of meeting Bear again one day.

Adithi writes books, film scripts and plays. Her YA novel, *Candid Tales: India on a Motorcycle*, made it to the Parag Honour List 2021. Her short stories and feature articles have appeared in American literary journals, and in anthologies by leading Indian publishing houses. You can find her at www.adithirao.com.

Aaryama Somayaji has studied Communication Design at the National Institute of Design, Vijayawada. She draws to survive, reads for herself, and eats to stay happy. Illustrating for children is her way of giving back the joy she had as a child. She lives in Delhi with her sibling and parents, much to their collective chagrin.

HAVALDAR HOOK
WANTS SOME ANSWERS

SOUND WORDS, also known as onomatopoeia, are where the sound suggests the sense. For example, the WHOOSH of the wind, the DUM of a drum and the CLINK of coins.

Match the pictures below to the sound words on the facing page.

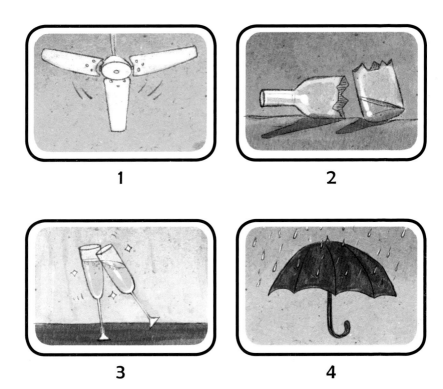

1

2

3

4